Editor: Nicole Lanctot
Production manager: Louise Kurtz
Designer: Ada Rodriguez

First published in the United States of America in 2015 by Abbeville Press,
137 Varick Street, New York, NY 10013

First published in Belgium in 2015 by Editions Mijade,
18, rue de l'ouvrage, 5000 Namur

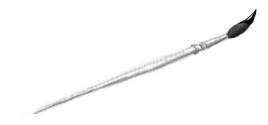

First edition
10 9 8 7 6 5 4 3 2 1

ISBN 978-0-7892-1246-7

Library of Congress Cataloging-in-Publication Data available upon request

For bulk and premium sales and for text adoption procedures, write to Customer
Service Manager, Abbeville Press, 137 Varick Street, New York, NY 10013,
or call 1-800-Artbook.

Visit Abbeville Press online at www.abbeville.com.

Zoe the Zebra

Sylviane Gangloff

Abbeville Kids
A DIVISION OF ABBEVILLE PRESS
New York · London

Hello!
My name is Zoe.

And I am the fastest zebra in the world!

Clippityclop! Clippityclop!

lippityclop!

Oh, no!
Where have my stripes gone?

Yoohoo!

Stripes, where are you?

Booohoo!

Everyone is going to make fun of me!

Has anyone seen my stripes?

Who's there?

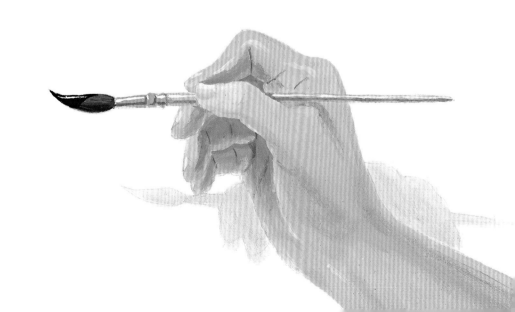

Hey! What are you doing?
What is this, anyway?

No,
I want stripes!
Not those!

He really doesn't understand.
A zebra must have stripes!

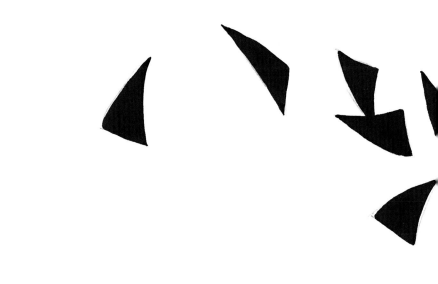

No!

No!

No!

You understand!
What a relief…

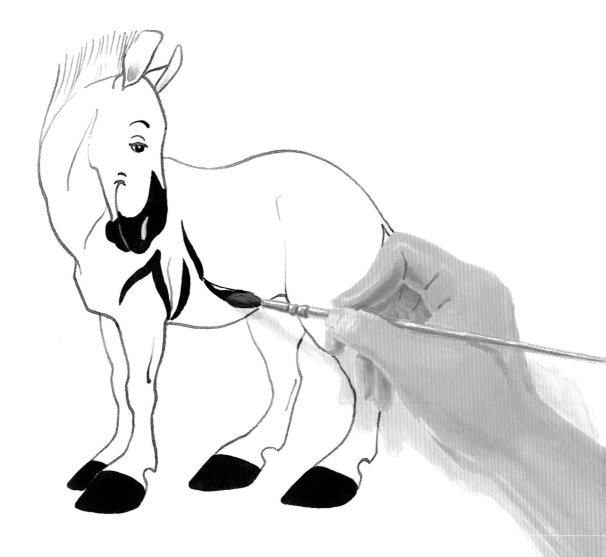

Snarl!
Now he's making fun of me!

And besides,
it's not easy to erase!

I want MY STRIPES and nothing else!

This time, I'm watching you!

Ah, my stripes!

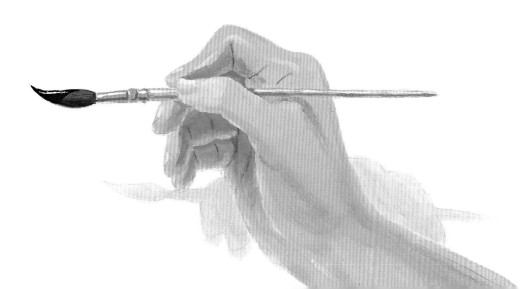

Now I can get zooming again…

Good-bye!

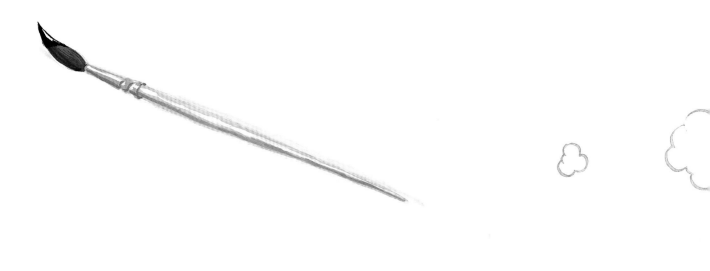